DEAD END

DEAD END

by

Liza Frenette

Illustrated by

Jane Gillis

North Country Books, Inc.
Utica, New York

DEAD END

Illustrated by Jane Gillis

ISBN 1-59531-001-0

Library of Congress Cataloging-in-Publication Data

Frenette, Liza, 1958-
Dead end / by Liza Frenette ; illustrated by Jane Gillis.
p. cm.
Summary: On an overnight group hike in the Adirondacks, Bridget
and her friends plan an elaborate joke to outwit the boys on the
trip,
but nothing can prepare them for the frightening sight not far from
their tents.
ISBN 1-59531-001-0 (alk. paper)
[1. Camping--Fiction. 2. Hiking--Fiction. 3. Adirondack Mountains
(N.Y.)--Fiction.] I. Gillis, Jane, ill. II. Title.
PZ7.F88935Dea 2005
[Fic]--dc22

2005010220

North Country Books, Inc.
311 Turner Street
Utica, New York 13501

This book is dedicated

to some real characters in my life:

Willie and Charlie Bencze

Bridget and Gretchen O'Leary

Gracey, Peter, and Annie Frenette

Thanks for the love, the stories, and the fun.

Contents

Acknowledgements

Thanks to my mother, Susanne Hull Frenette, for taking us up Mount Arab every Wednesday in the summer while we stayed at "camp." Thanks to my dad, James Frenette, for making camp possible and bringing us on outdoor adventures all the time.

Thanks to Woody, the ranger in the fire tower at Mount Arab.

Thanks to my hardy readers, proofreaders, and idea givers, especially Rosemarie Kent, Nancy and Lucy Castaldo, Lois Feister Huey, Jennifer Groff and Coleen Paratore, from our wonderful "Writers on Wednesday" group. They are tremendously helpful to me.

Thanks to Michaela Tompkins for her great reading and voice. Thanks to "Hurricane" Haley Korn for cheering me on.

Thanks for the Friends of Mount Arab, including Uncle Bill Frenette, for helping to keep a great place going.

Thanks to my tribe: Rosemarie Guidice, Diane Cyr, Maisie Thompson, Lori Martin, Charlie Miller, Gerry Colborn, Karen "Stone" Sleight, Sue Okun, Darci D'Ercole, Anna Sid, Jane Milner, Claudia Ricci, Linda

Hogan, Jackie Moore and her late husband George, Mary Bergquist, Liz Fitzgerald, my sweet cousin Nadine Hull Lauer, Mike Lennon, Peter B. and Bill's friends.

For Leonard Richard Schwartz for reading my work with such eagerness, and for love and support in low tide muck.

To the memory of Rick Sack, who was a healer of many gifts and much love; thanks for still showing up as the red-tailed hawk. We need you.

For healers Cathy Reamer, Joanna Stellato-Kabat, and Dr. Emily LaJeunesse.

Thanks to my sisters Sarah Bencze and Margaret O'Leary, both teachers, who keep outdoor education going strong.

To the memory of our longtime great neighbor, Florentine Camelo.

Thanks to my fun and inspiring colleagues at New York Teacher and in media relations at New York State United Teachers.

To North Country Books for supporting children's literature.

And most importantly, for my family, Jasmine, and our dogs, Ming and Simon, of course.

Chapter One

Packing Secrets

Flashlight. Rain poncho. Bug spray. A great new mystery to read. Water bottle. Chocolate. Granola bars. Sweatshirt. Socks. And the special book, at the bottom of the backpack, covered in brown paper from a grocery bag so that no one would see the title.

Bridget went through her backpack for the umpteenth time to make sure she had everything for the hiking trip. Then she added her long johns, just in case. It could get very cold during the night in the fall—especially on top of an Adirondack mountain. Her sleeping bag was tied to the bottom of her pack with rope. Her mom would be carrying the pup tent.

The phone rang and Bridget jumped off her bed and clomped down the hall in her hiking boots to answer it. Ming followed, her bushy tail waving back and forth. Then her mom opened her bedroom door and started down the hall.

"I got it!" Bridget said as she reached the stand in the hallway.

She picked up the phone. "Anna, don't worry, we're almost ready!"

"How did you know it was me?"

"Hey, best friends just know stuff about each other. Like I know your full name is Anna Susanne Hull, so your initials spell ASH."

"Okay, just keep that to yourself," Anna said, groaning. "Listen, I'm all packed, and so's my mom." She lowered her voice. "I have the magnifying glass. I also have the fold-out map of Adirondack animal tracks, and it's the new edition with the moose tracks on it."

"Great!" Bridget squealed.

"Shhh!" Anna said. "We can't let on."

"Okay, okay. We'll be in your driveway in ten minutes."

She hung up the phone, smiling. She couldn't wait to see them: Anna, her younger sisters Gracey and Gretchen, and their mom. They were all going for an overnight hike up Mount Arab. Their neighbors, Willie and Charlie, their mom, and another friend Peter were also joining them.

Willie and Charlie were really good hikers, and they had a lot of experience in the woods. It would be good to have them along.

But they also liked to brag about all the wild and brave things they'd done and seen, and Anna and Bridget were pretty sure they made up some of their stories. Last week at the school's first "Show and Tell" of the year, Charlie had come dressed in a fur hat with a skunk tail hanging off the back of it. He told everyone how he'd found this sick skunk dying in the woods about a mile back from his house.

"I took care of that skunk for three days and three nights, and it never sprayed me," Charlie told the class. "When he died, I was at his side. I figured it was the right thing to do to save his tail and wear it proudly. So I cut it off with my hunting knife, and buried the skunk."

Anna and Bridget had looked at each other with "I don't think so" looks.

That's when they started thinking of a plan for the hiking trip. They were sure that even though Willie and Charlie had seen a lot of animals during their hiking and camping trips, they'd never seen a moose. So on this trip, the girls were going to make sure those boys thought they spotted signs of a moose. They'd be sure to brag to everyone back at school, and then Bridget and Anna would bust them.

Bridget went back to her room and hauled her backpack downstairs. She didn't know how she would ever carry it up Mount Arab. It felt so heavy.

But she was really psyched. Aside from the plan to trick Willie and Charlie, Bridget was excited about climbing a mountain. She picked up Ming, her black and white shih tzu, and looked right at her. "We're going to go camping, Ming, and I'm going to climb a real fire tower on top of the mountain!" Ming tilted her head toward Bridget. "You can't go up the tower, no, it's too dangerous," she said to the dog. "I wonder if it will be scary?"

She put Ming down and looked at her watch.

"Come on Mom!" she hollered upstairs. "We're late."

"I can't find my keys," her mom shouted. She came downstairs and started looking through a pile of stuff on the kitchen counter. Then she began lifting the chair and couch cushions, and then she started raising her voice, just like she told Bridget not to.

"Where are the keys? I can't find the keys!" she said, sounding panicky.

Bridget rolled her eyes, and then started helping her mother look. How was she always losing her keys? Sometimes her mother drove her crazy.

Ming scurried over to the front door, and sniffed the food in Bridget's backpack. When Bridget went to get the dog away from the food, she noticed her mom's keys hanging on the wall. On the key rack. Right next to the front door. She picked them up, sighed, and dangled them in her hand for her mother to see. It was high time to get this show on the road; the moose are calling.

Chapter Two

Grooved Pavement

"Hey, three girls in the back, two moms in front, one baby in the middle seat!" Gracey said, clapping. "3-2-1!" They were all stuffed in one car, heading to the mountain. They'd meet Willie, Charlie, Mrs. Bends, and the boys' friend, Peter, at the trailhead.

Seated in the middle of the back seat, Gracey nudged Anna with one elbow and then Bridget with the other, laughing.

"Come on guys, let's eat our snacks now!" she said. "No, wait. Let's play 'My Grandmother's Trunk.' I'll start. I opened my grandmother's trunk and inside there were antlers. Now Bridget it's your turn to find something in the trunk that starts with "B," and you have to say that plus my word, antlers. Then Anna, you have to find something that starts with a "C" and we just keep on going."

"We know how to play," said Anna, rolling her eyes. They began the game, but by the time they got to the letter "K," Gracey wanted to play something else. She and Anna began fighting.

"Don't be *acrimonious*," blurted out Bridget.

"Huh?" Anna asked.

"Oh, you know, it means to fight bitterly, or something like that," said Bridget, turning to look out the window, shrugging.

This time, it was Gracey who rolled her eyes. "Let's have some food!" she said.

They unzipped their packs and pulled out chocolate bars and sour balls.

"How come you don't come over after school anymore?" Anna asked Bridget.

"Oh, I've just been studying, I guess," Bridget said. Then she stuffed a piece of candy in her mouth so she wouldn't have to talk anymore. She was studying, that much was true, but it wasn't about getting ahead—except Anna didn't know that.

Just then, the car's tires started making funny noises as they passed over a section of road that was being replaced. It felt like there were ridges in the pavement. Orange cones lined the roadside, along with signs to slow down. Bridget looked out her window and saw one large road sign that said "Grooved Pavement." She nudged her friends.

"Hey, grooved pavement!" she said. "A bunch of hippies must live near here."

Gracey looked at her with her face scrunched up, not understanding what Bridget meant.

"Okay, you know how me and my dad always make up stories about road signs?" Bridget asked. "Well, if it says grooved pavement, it's a secret code to let us know that hippies live here. They say 'groovy' all the time!"

Her mom laughed.

The road became smooth again, and the girls dove back into their candy.

Bridget was trading candy with Gracey when she heard her mother say the name "Joe," and then saw her mother turn and smile at Mrs. Hull. Then she whispered, and Bridget knew she heard the word "boyfriend."

Then her mother actually blushed!

Gross.

Bridget got very quiet. She looked out the window again.

So, her mother must really like Joe, a guy who worked at the local college. Bridget knew her mom had a few dates with him while she was overnight at her dad's house. Then her mom had him over to dinner—twice—and last week, he sent her mother flowers. They were fancy flowers from a florist, too, not just some wildflowers like her mother was always growing for her part-time summer job planting rock gardens for people.

Since then, he'd been calling the house every day. That's probably why her mom came out into the hall so quickly today when the phone rang, her mom must've been hoping it was Joe on the phone.

Bridget knew her mom had guy friends, especially since she worked for the Department of Transportation operating a snowplow in the winter. Mrs. Meagher worked with a lot of guys. And she knew that since her mother and father had been divorced a few years now, they'd each had some dates.

But Bridget had never before seen her mother actually blush while talking about a guy.

And she'd certainly never heard her call a guy a "boyfriend." She squirmed in her seat. She didn't want her mother to have a boyfriend. No way. It was too embarrassing. Boyfriends weren't for moms. It was a stupid name, for one thing; guys her mom's age weren't boys.

Plus, she and Anna might have boyfriends any day now; after all, they were already twelve. There was even a kid in Bridget's class that she liked talking to. He was cute, and he liked to read, just like she did. Not that she wanted to date. But come on, how could she even think about it when her own mother was blushing over a boyfriend?

"Hey, over there, Bridget! Are you still on Planet Earth?" Anna looked across Gracey to find Bridget's face.

"Yeah," said Bridget, shaking her head as if to clear it. "I'll tell you what. Before we get to the trailhead, it's time to finish working out our plans to bust Willie and Charlie ."

And the three girls began whispering again, and pulled out their stash of clay supplies from a bag they'd hidden in the car.

"We'll let those guys see what a Show and Tell is really like," Anna said. "This is one show they won't soon forget!"

Chapter Three

To the Top

The towns seemed to get smaller and the trees bigger as they drove to Mount Arab. From their house on the backside of Whiteface Mountain, it took about an hour and a half to drive there, past Saranac Lake, Tupper Lake, Piercefield, and then Conifer, a tiny town named after types of evergreen trees that all have cones. The town had once been filled with homes of lumberjacks and loggers who worked in the woods cutting down trees for lumber and paper products. Now it was just an echo of a town with a few houses here and there, back in the trees.

"Hey, we're here," Mrs. Hull said finally, as they turned into a small dirt parking lot. A marker at the bottom of the trail announced that this was Mount Arab. Willie, Charlie, Mrs. Bends, and Peter were already there. They stood ready, packs on their backs, waving and waiting. Willie wore a bright orange jacket, and Peter had on a football jersey and a leftover Fourth of July baseball hat with battery-operated lights that look like fireworks. Charlie had on his skunk-tail hat.

"He'll get pretty hot hiking with that stupid thing on," Anna said to

Bridget, pointing to Charlie as they got out of the car.

"And, Peter will sure scare off any moose with that crazy hat," Bridget whispered. They looked at each other, shrugged and giggled.

They hoisted their packs onto their backs and walked to the trailhead.

"Hey guys," they all greeted each other. "Hi, Mrs. Bends," Bridget said to Willie and Charlie's mom.

"I hope you're ready to hike with the best of 'em," Willie bragged. "The first one up to the top of the fire tower gets a special prize."

"What is it?" Gracey asked. "I want to drink a really, really cold soda at the top. How about that as the prize? Can you keep a soda cold on a hike? I hate it when they get all warm and taste like dish soap."

"Now, how would you know what dish soap tastes like, Gracey?" Peter asked.

Everyone laughed, even Gracey.

"It's better than soap, Gracey, don't worry, but it's a surprise," said Charlie. "How about your skunk-tail hat? Can that be the prize?" Anna asked, laughing.

"Go ahead and laugh, you're just jealous," Charlie said, adjusting his hat.

"Hey," Willie shouted, "Before we go up, did you guys see the sign at the end of this road? You better check it out."

The girls walked back to the cars and looked down the road. A short way off was a bright yellow road sign that said "Dead End."

"Yeah," Charlie said, grinning, "So you better not be dead last at the end of the hike! Get it?"

"Okay, get moving guys," said their mom. "Come on everybody. It's a gorgeous day."

They all headed up the trail, with Gretchen in the backpack her mom carried. Her curly hair was as red as the sugar maple leaves that had already turned color for fall.

Bridget breathed in deeply to smell the pine and balsam. It was such a comforting, earthy smell. She loved being in the woods, even though she and Gracey had once gotten lost in the woods in back of their house in a snowstorm. That had been scary. Another time, she and her friends had to help carry a sick girl a long way out of the woods, near a remote falls. It seemed like the woods always held adventure and promise, as well as both good and bad memories.

The trip would also give her stuff to write about for her different classes. School was tougher, now that she was in her second year of middle school. And boy had she ever learned that last week . . .

"Aaaaaa!" Gretchen suddenly screamed, pointing down.

"Look!" said Anna. "It's only a salamander."

"That critter sure can scitter," said Willie.

"Ohhhhh! I want to catch it," Gracey said, scooting around to try and grab the reddish-colored amphibian squiggling through the leaves. It was a tiny creature, low to the ground, with a small head and a very long tail. Ming sniffed at it, encouraging the salamander to move even faster.

"You better hold off, Gracey. We have nowhere to keep it and I'm sure you wouldn't want it crawling around in your sleeping bag," Willie said.

At that thought, Gracey stopped in her tracks. She turned toward the trail again and started climbing.

" 'Salamander' comes from a Greek word meaning 'fire-lizard,' " said

Mrs. Hull. Bridget smiled; she could always tell Anna's mom was a teacher.

"Seeing a salamander is great, but wouldn't it be even greater if we saw a moose?" Bridget asked, winking at Anna.

The boys stopped and looked at each other.

"Hey…" Willie said.

"This would be the right time of year to see one," Anna interupted. "They roam a lot in fall because that's when they look for mates."

"Yeah, in the summer they mostly hang out by the water to stay cool," said Bridget.

"How do you guys know so much about moose?" Willie asked.

"Where have you been? Everybody knows there's a lot of moose in the Adirondacks," said Bridget. "You must know a lot about them, since you guys are always in the woods. Haven't you ever seen one?"

"No," Charlie said, frowning.

"I bet you haven't either," said Peter, sticking out his chin.

"No, not yet," said Gracey, smiling, "but you never know."

"Anyway, you'd scare more than a moose away with those blinking lights on your hat," Bridget laughed. She smiled at Peter; they were good friends, even if he did look weird. She shouldn't be surprised, though: last year for Halloween he'd dressed up as a cheerleader, with a dress, a wig, and pom-poms.

They kept on hiking, going further and further uphill. A soft wind blew through the trees, but the air was hot. Ming was panting a lot and Bridget had to stop to give her water from a collapsible bowl she'd put in her backpack.

When she looked up, she saw the boys going onto a side path off the main trail. It was the second time they'd done that today.

"Will you guys stay on the path. You're being so…so…*capricious*!" Bridget said, wiping her bangs from her sweaty forehead.

They stared at her.

"It means changing suddenly, like you just keep changing paths," she said.

"What are you, Miss Smarty Hiker?" Willie asked.

"Boys, you know you should stay on the main trail. It's dangerous to stray," said their mom. "And follow these round red trail markers that you always need to look for while you're hiking in the woods. Stay on the trail with the markers, no fooling around."

As they started hiking again, Gracey tugged on Bridget's sleeve.

"Hey, Bridget, I've got a secret sign story," she said.

"Okay, what is it?"

"Listen," Gracey said, stopping in the middle of the path. "'Trail marker.' It's a new kind of marking pen that you can use to draw trails when you're making maps and stuff! That's what it secretly means!"

"Not bad, Sis," Anna said.

"Hey," said Willie, "That reminds me. Last week I went to a friend's house, he lives in one of those new developments. They put those things in the road so you have to slow down while you're driving, and the sign said 'SPEED HUMPS.' You should tell your dad, Bridget, that it means you must have to watch out for fast camels!"

Everyone started laughing.

"Okay, guys, as long as we're stopped, everyone drink some water. It's important. Whew, these packs are heavy!" said Bridget's mom, resting on a rock.

As they climbed, the trail got steeper and rockier. Anna's mom had to rest a few times from the weight of carrying Gretchen. The baby loved reaching up from her backpack and trying to grab leaves off the trees.

They spotted a tree with a wide opening in the middle of its trunk, like the wind had tunneled right through it.

"Hey, Anna, take my picture," Bridget said, sticking her face in the hole. "Then I can send it to Jasmine. It will look like I'm a tree person."

Anna put down her pack and pulled out her camera and took a picture while Bridget made a silly face. Jasmine was Bridget's pen pal and friend from Cape Cod that she'd met while vacationing there with her mom. They saw each other every summer.

Then they kept on hiking, and kept on sweating. Squirrels chattered as they raced up and down tree trunks, getting as much food as they could before winter set in. Every so often, yellow leaves gently twirled down through the air, then red ones, then orange.

Finally, through the thickness of the thousands of leaves still on the trees, Bridget could see the sky. She knew they were getting near the top. Bridget was really glad about that, because she sure was getting tired.

As they neared the top, the boys began sprinting. There was no way Bridget could catch them. She was lucky to be able to climb up the last slope. Her legs were feeling kind of mushy.

At the summit, Willie, Charlie, and Peter had grins nearly as wide as the sky. They had planted a little flag made from a stick and one of Peter's ripped-up T-shirts.

"We're the kings of the mountain!" Peter shouted.

"Hey, you might beat us up to the top, but we always beat you in school, right, Bridget?" Anna hollered down to Bridget as she struggled up the last few steps. "Bridget and I always tie for the smartest in our class."

Bridget didn't answer. Didn't Anna know it wasn't cool to brag about grades? Besides, she couldn't exactly boast about that right now. She hadn't told anyone about the test she'd gotten back two weeks ago—certainly not her mom, and certainly, not even Anna.

Bridget huffed and puffed, and planted her hiking boots firmly on the smooth rock until she stood, finally, totally out in the open, with the mountain breeze washing over her skin like a wind shower. Her hair flew free. All around her she could see more mountains, and several wide blue lakes beneath them.

"Aha, the kingdom of the magnificent!" Bridget shouted. "This is so great!"

"If this is a kingdom, then I want to be the queen," pronounced Gracey, very seriously.

"It's done. You shall be queen," said Bridget. "I shall make you a crown of leaves, just like in *Bridge to Terabithia*, one of my most favorite books."

"Can I read it someday, too?" asked Gracey, as Bridget searched for long branches of leaves to wrap into a crown.

They started whooping and shouting as their moms made it up to the top behind them. Mrs. Hull eased her backpack down off her shoulders and took Gretchen out of the pack.

Soon everyone was laughing and breaking out candy bars, juicy oranges, and water bottles. Charlie squirted water right in his face to cool off. He even took off his hat. They all sat on the rocks, enjoying the breeze and looking at all the beauty surrounding them. They could see Mt. Arab Lake and Eagle Crag Lake, which looked like an eagle standing with its wings folded behind it.

"There, in the east, you can see the Adirondack High Peaks," said Mrs. Bends. "We've climbed lots of those mountains, haven't we guys?"

"Yup," agreed Willie and Charlie in unison.

"And there's Mount Morris over there, where I spent all my free time skiing when I was growing up," said Mrs. Meagher. "Remember, Bridget, I took you to the ski slope there before it closed?"

"Yeah, I remember falling all the time," Bridget laughed.

"What a great clear day," said Mrs. Bends. "I wish the boys' father were here; he'd love this."

"Yeah, I wish Joe could see this," said Mrs. Meagher.

Bridget scowled. She'd rather have her father here, and she wasn't ready to share any family outing with Joe.

She turned away from them to look at the fire tower. They'd climb that next. Willie and Charlie had been climbing mountains with fire towers all summer in order to earn a special "Fire Tower" patch from the Adirondack Mountain Club. They were almost done.

Bridget arched her neck to stare up at the metal steps reaching to the top of the tower, where there was a wood and glass booth with someone inside. It looked very, very high, and very, very scary.

Chapter Four

One Secret Gets Spilled

"Okay gang, I want to set up camp before we go up the tower," said Mrs. Bends.

"But Mom…" replied Willie, "We want to climb the tower."

"We're setting up camp first. Once you're up in that tower, you'll be there forever," she said.

While the boys were off finding a spot for the tents, Bridget asked Mrs. Hull to watch Ming. "We have a mission," she whispered. Then the girls quietly ran a short way down the trail they'd just climbed.

Last week they had made a mold out of clay that would leave the imprint of a moose track. They took it out of the backpack, carefully pushing it into the dirt over and over again so it would look like a bunch of tracks leading into the bushes.

"This looks totally real," said Anna, clapping.

They unwrapped a plastic bag of brown, round clay balls they had made and stashed in the car. They put them in a pile to make them look like moose droppings, and then began giggling so hard at what they were doing that Bridget's stomach ached from trying not to laugh too loud.

"Just think, we hiked up a mountain with moose poop in our packs!" Gracey giggled.

They began laughing all over again.

Not far from the tracks, they bent some bushes to make it look like they'd been trampled, and then picked up some branches that had already fallen and snapped them.

"Just lay them around on the ground so it looks like a moose has crashed through here," said Bridget.

"Looks good," Anna said when they were done. "Let's get back before they notice we're gone." They quietly walked back up the trail, squatting as they got closer to the clearing so the boys wouldn't spot them.

They scooted up the rock and were back on top of the mountain just as the boys came back from a small clearing in the woods on the other side of the mountain.

"Good job, girls. We've been quite *intrepid*," Bridget whispered to the sisters.

"What's with you and these big fat words all of a sudden?" Anna asked.

This time, Bridget blushed.

"Nothing," she said.

Anna stared at her.

"I've known you forever, and you're going to stand here and tell me 'Nothing'?" Anna said, planting her feet firmly on the ground.

"Never mind," Bridget said. "Here come the guys."

"We found a great spot, so lug your gear over here," Willie announced, waving to them. In the distance, Bridget could see the moms unloading tents in the clearing.

They started to follow the boys, but then Bridget suddenly turned to Anna and Gracey and said, “Wait, let’s go up the fire tower now while they’re walking the other way. Then we can beat them to the top.”

The three of them raced to the bottom of the tower and began climbing the metal stairs. Each set of stairs had a landing and then a turn to another set of stairs. The higher they climbed, the more the wind tugged at them. The wind kept slapping Bridget’s hair into her eyes. She was first in line, and she held the railing tightly. The wind made her feel like one of those leaves that had fallen from the trees today, like she, too, could get blown around by it

“I feel like we’re climbing to the clouds,” Bridget said. “We should have ditched our packs before going up here, it’d be easier.”

“Never mind, just keep going,” encouraged Gracey, who was holding onto her sister’s hand.

From below, Bridget saw her mom wave to her, but she didn’t dare let go of the railing and wave back. Her mom walked over to the tower and began climbing. Bridget was secretly glad her mom would be behind them; this was scary.

“My mom won’t come up,” said Anna. “She’s afraid of heights. Plus, she’d never come up with Gretchen.”

They climbed until they reached the floor of the tower. Bridget lifted up her hand and knocked. A young woman opened up the door in the floor of the tower.

"Hey, come on in, it's nice to have some company," she said. "Welcome aboard! I'm Sarah."

Since it was a tight fit to get inside, Bridget took her pack off her back to give to the woman, but just as she did a gust of wind grabbed it right out of her hand.

"Oh no," she cried, watching as the pack plunged to the ground. She watched it hit the rocks far below, and winced.

"Anything breakable in there?" asked Sarah, holding out her hand to Bridget.

"No, well, I don't think so," Bridget said.

"Hey, don't worry, we'll get it when we go back down," said her mom, coming up behind the girls.

"And girls, you should have told me you were going up the tower. I know you wanted to beat the guys, but it's important to follow the rules. The plan was to get the tents set up first, and you knew that."

"I'm sorry, Mom," Bridget said. "We just raced up here without thinking. We'll get the tents set up as soon as we get down, and help with dinner, too. I promise."

Bridget stepped inside, and soon was followed by Anna, Gracey, and then her mom. They moved to the back of the tower, while the woman shut the door in the floor.

"That's all there's room for now," Sarah said.

"Good, that means no boys allowed," Gracey said. "This can be a girls clubhouse for now." She turned to Sarah. "I can't believe you have a floor-door. I wish I had one like that in my bedroom because it's right over

the kitchen. I could open it up and hop down onto the refrigerator!"

Bridget's mom hugged Gracey. "You think of everything," she said.

Yeah, not everybody thinks about Joe, Bridget thought.

Sarah told them how she was one of a group of volunteer stewards for the fire tower.

"Come on, take a look at my world," she said.

From the moment Bridget looked out the window, she forgot about her pack, her mother's boyfriend, school, and the moose tracks. She couldn't take her eyes off the scenery. Spread out all around and beneath them were mountains, trees with leaves turning the warm colors of fall, and sparkling blue lakes. The wind blew at the tower, but they were safe. They were high above the world.

"It's like a magic kingdom," Gracey whispered.

"Look, you can even see the Raquette River from here," said Sarah, handing out binoculars. "And there's Gull Pond."

She showed them the map table and alidad, the device she used to survey the area and determine the exact location of everything she could see from the tower.

"This way, if I see smoke or suspect a fire, I know exactly where it's coming from, and I can call on my radio. There are only twenty-eight fire towers left on all the mountains in New York, and only a few of them are still staffed."

"Why?" asked Anna.

"Well, many of them were taken down because some hikers didn't believe they belonged in wilderness areas," Sarah said. "It's really too bad.

Towers were first put up after great fires in the early 1900s destroyed nearly a million acres of Adirondack forest."

"That's a lot of trees," said Bridget.

"There was always someone in the tower here when I was growing up," Mrs. Meagher explained. "We used to have a summer camp on the Raquette River and my mom took us up this mountain every week while my dad was at work. There was a guy named Woody in the tower then. We all knew him."

"Hey, Mom, I didn't know you got to hang out with a ranger in a fire tower," Bridget said. "That's cool."

"We always looked forward to seeing Woody. He knew all of us. We used to camp up here sometimes, too; that's how I thought of this trip."

"Sure, I remember hearing about Woody," Sarah said. "He worked here for many years."

Out another window, Sarah showed them a small cabin below they hadn't noticed. "A volunteer group called The Friends of Mount Arab is fixing up that cabin. That was where Woody stayed years ago before the cabin was left to deteriorate. The same group put on a new roof, windows, and floor in this tower."

"What a wonderful group," exclaimed Mrs. Meagher.

"Geez, can you imagine staying up here all alone in a cabin every night on top of a mountain?" Bridget asked.

"No way," Gracey said, shivering. "That's too scary."

Just then there was a knock on the floor. Gracey jumped.

"I think it's time to let in the next crew," Sarah said. "No one will be here in the tower tomorrow, unfortunately, because we have to rely on volunteers. It's good you guys made your hike today. I'll be leaving myself in a little while."

"Thanks, Sarah," they said.

She opened the door, and saw the boys waiting to come in. They stepped against the railing to make room for the girls to climb out, one at a time, followed by Bridget's mom.

"Hey, I get the prize," Bridget bragged, with a smug smile, standing on the landing. "I was first up the tower."

She held out her hand.

"Hurry up," she said. "It's windy and I don't want to drop it."

"Sure thing, Miss Smarty Hiker," Willie said, nudging the other two boys. "Since you already dropped everything else."

"Yeah, Miss Big Word Hiker," teased Peter.

Bridget wondered why they were teasing her about her big words.

"Just give me the prize," she said. Peter dropped a package into her hands. They all began laughing when Bridget saw that they had given her a whoopee cushion that could make noises like farts if you blew it up and then sat on it to squish it.

Bridget laughed too, stuck it in her pocket and then carefully, slowly climbed back down the tower.

At the bottom, she walked toward where she thought her pack had fallen. At first, she couldn't spot it. But then she saw all her stuff was strewn about everywhere. Her sweatshirt was in a nearby bush. Her flashlight was broken.

"I can't believe this!" she cried to Anna and Gracey. She stomped around picking up her things; tears stinging her eyes, and not from the wind anymore. She felt a knot in her stomach.

"Argh, this stinks," she yelled.

As Bridget picked up her things, she realized something was missing. The knot in her stomach felt tighter. Bridget wished she could be alone right now. She just wanted to cry really hard. Where was her book?

"What's the matter?" Gracey asked, twirling a piece of her hair nervously around her finger.

"I, uh, I just thought I was missing something else," Bridget said.

"Like THIS?" shouted Charlie from behind them, standing at the bottom landing of the fire tower stairs, dangling a book in his hands. The brown paper wrapper was torn; and the book was in a couple different sections where it had broken apart when it hit the ground.

"Yeah, Miss Smarty Hiker, now we know why you're so brainy!" Peter said. "You carry around a dictionary! Your secret is OUT OF THE BAG, get it?"

"Yeah, who brings a dictionary CAMPING?" Willie teased.

"Oh, I know," Charlie said, opening the book. "You probably needed to look up the word tent—T-E-N-T. It means a shelter used to go camping in, usually made of nylon or canvas."

The boys started laughing.

Bridget was so mad she felt like throwing a rock at them. Instead she stomped her foot, yelled "SHUT UP," grabbed her backpack filled with what was left of her stuff, and ran off. She wouldn't cry in front of them, no way. She wrapped her arms around herself to keep from crying, because she knew once she let loose, she would cry really hard.

She ran down a path. She couldn't stand boys. She would never, ever date them, no matter what. Her mother could have all the boyfriends she wanted, but she never would, no way. And now everyone would know her secret.

Chapter Five

Shelter in the Rocks

Bridget ran over to their campsite and quickly took Ming by her leash. Her mom and Mrs. Bends were getting out the cookware, and Mrs. Hull was feeding Gretchen, so nobody noticed her.

Normally, Bridget liked setting up camp, but not now.

Now she needed to be alone.

She went a couple of feet down the back of the mountain and sat huddled in a crevice, then she pulled Ming onto her lap and petted her. The tears came. They were hot. They stung her face, right along with the wind. She didn't care. She buried her face into Ming. He always knew when she was upset.

Bridget looked out over the lakes far below. They sparkled in the late afternoon sun. The wind blew at her; at first it seemed to whirl around in the ache she felt inside, like there was a lot of empty space in there.

Slowly, slowly the warmth of her dog filled that space. The wind started to blow away all her rocky thoughts about failing her spelling test, about how confusing it was in middle school with so many more kids than there was in her elementary school in Bloomingdale, about the boys discovering her dictionary, about her ruined stuff, and about her mom probably having a boyfriend. She took out a broken chocolate bar from the bag and ate that, and then she gave Ming a dog treat. The dog licked Bridget's face, and she gave the shih tzu a big hug.

She started to feel a little better. She decided that it was time to tell Anna about how she had failed her test, and why she was lugging a dictionary up a mountain. Bridget took Ming off her lap, and stood up to go back to the campsite. She pulled a sweatshirt out of her pack and yanked it over her head to warm herself. Walking carefully on the rocky trail, she had only gone a few feet when she found Anna sitting by herself under a tree.

"Why are you always running away when you get upset?" Anna asked, looking up at her.

Bridget took a deep breath.

"I wasn't, I guess. I don't know, I just wanted to be by myself," Bridget answered.

She sat down next to Anna.

"See, sometimes I don't figure things out by myself. My mom tries to figure them out for me, or my dad. Or even you. But I didn't want to tell any of you about this, because it was just such an awful mess, so I thought if I took care of it by myself no one would have to know," Bridget explained.

"What'd you do, rob a bank?"

Bridget laughed. "Doubt it," she said.

"What, then?"

"I flunked a test. A really big test on spelling and reading comprehension."

Anna stared at her. “You, the best reader I know, flunked a test on that?”

“Yeah, I think I cried all night. I don’t know what happened. Well, I sort of know. I just hadn’t been studying. I didn’t think I had to.”

Bridget picked up a stick and drew circles around and around in the dirt and pine needles. She didn’t look at Anna.

“Sometimes, I just want to hang out with the other kids. I mean, come on, we live out in the middle of nowhere and don’t get to see anyone our age after school. So in study hall, I’ve been writing notes and stuff instead of doing homework. Then, at night, I’ve been talking a lot on the phone with kids in my class—that is, until the big “F” came along. I’m so afraid I’m going to get grounded.”

“Well, you can study with me,” Anna said. “We can hang out at night. I’m right next door. Unless you’re sick of me or something.”

“No, I’m not,” Bridget said, finally looking straight at Anna. “I just started out this year thinking I’d make new friends. It wasn’t that I don’t want to hang with you. I just wanted to get to know more people and not work so much. But I didn’t know how much harder getting an ‘F’ would be.”

“Yeah, I bet.”

“But Anna, I never failed a test in my life before, not ever. And I don’t ever want to again. I didn’t want you to know, because it was embarrassing.”

“So you went and bought a dictionary and read it every night for the past two weeks like one of your novels?” Anna asked, looking wide-eyed at Bridget. “That’s why you haven’t been coming over?

Bridget leaned over and hugged Anna.

"You're still my best friend for sure," Bridget said. "Now don't make me feel like a total geek about the dictionary."

"So you've been studying it—in secret?"

"Like mad. Totally. Can you tell?"

Anna sighed. "Who could miss it? Come on, we better go *proffer* cooking assistance to our mothers, or we will be in *dire dinner doldrums*. How's that?"

They helped pull each other up from the ground, and then Bridget said, "You know, Anna, I wouldn't be able to tell any of the other girls at school about this. I'm glad I could tell you, even if it took me awhile. Thanks."

"Sure. Next time don't wait for things to come crashing down from a fire tower before you tell me."

They ran back to the campsite, where they pulled their sleeping bags out of their stuff sacks and set up their pup tent.

"I'm sleeping with you guys, too, right?" Gracey asked, coming over to help.

"Sure, we can all squeeze in," said Bridget.

"And Ming, too?"

"Yes, Ming too."

"I'm sorry you were upset about your backpack. Would you like to wear my crown of leaves to cheer you up?"

"Oh thanks, Gracey," said Bridget, giving Gracey a hug. "I'm all right now."

"Look," said Gracey, holding out a plastic container with a lid. "The boys trapped a bee in this. I let it go. Everyone picks on bees and wants to kill them. I'm going to start a club called Free The Bees! You know, like Save the Whales. Do you want to be a member?"

"Well...I guess so."

"We can make the fire tower our secret clubhouse," Gracey whispered.

"Come on girls, help us fix dinner," Mrs. Bends called. "We sent the boys out to find kindling and firewood."

While they were shucking corn, Gracey snuck a brownie, and marched around chanting, "Free the Bees! Free the Bees!" They wrapped the corn in aluminum foil to cook in the fire. Later, they'd heat up tortillas with beans, cheese, and the rice Mrs. Hull had brought.

Bridget went over to help feed Gretchen her mashed peas. She loved being with her, and often wished she had a baby sister.

"Hey, Gretchen girl," she said. "How're you doing on your first camping trip? Do you like the woods, huh? See all those trees?"

Gretchen looked up at her and smiled.

"Big," she said. "Big."

"Yeah, they're big trees," said Bridget.

Suddenly, they heard shouts from down the trail.

"Hey, you guys, come look!" Peter yelled, running up the path. "Willie and Charlie found moose tracks, you won't believe it!"

Chapter Six

Moose on the Loose

The girls looked at each with smiles as wide as the open trail on the mountaintop. They gave each other high fives and shouted, "Yes!"

"Okay, girls, what gives?" asked Bridget's mom.

"Well, remember that secret mission we had?" Anna answered. "We planted some fake moose tracks and droppings, because the boys are always bragging about their big adventures. We wanted them to think they spotted signs of a moose."

"You guys deserve each other," Mrs. Bends laughed. "They tease you, and you play tricks on them."

"We have to go see the tracks now, to pretend they're the real deal," Bridget said. Then she leaned toward Anna and whispered: "That is, until we get to school on Monday and tell everyone else they were totally fake."

"Well, take the flashlights. It won't be long before its dark," Mrs. Hull said.

Bridget took Ming, and she, Anna, and Gracey headed off to find them.

"Over here! Over here!" Peter yelled, waving his arms and racing back down the trail toward Willie and Charlie.

When they reached the boys, Willie and Charlie were huddled over the tracks.

"Check this out," Charlie shouted. "I know these are moose tracks. I just know it."

"Yeah," said Willie, "This is unbelievable."

They all squatted down to look.

"Let's make sure," said Anna, and she pulled out her guide of animal tracks from her back pocket and unfolded it. They all studied it together.

"They are! I knew it," cried Charlie, taking off his fur hat and slapping it on his leg.

"What's that?" asked Bridget, pointing to the nearby pile of brown balls.

"Ew! I think its moose poop!" said Gracey, winking at Bridget.

"Gross," said Willie, squatting in front of the pile. "It can't be that fresh, though, it doesn't seem to smell. Still, this makes it definite. Let's hunt around for some more tracks. I'm never gonna' sleep tonight, thinking about that moose wandering around."

"Hey," shouted Charlie. "Look, at these bushes. This thing must be huge. Come on, let's check it out."

They walked a ways into the woods, shining their flashlights in the underbrush darkened by the trees overhead and the fading light.

Peter pointed his light downward. "Look, more broken branches! That moose crashed through here! I can't wait to tell my sister. She'll sure be sorry she missed this camping trip."

"This is so awesome," said Willie.

Charlie had his flashlight low to the ground, looking for more clues.

"We can't go too far," reminded Anna. "We're off the trail. Remember the rules."

Charlie bent over, studying the ground, brushing here and there with his hand at the edge of some bushes. Then his hand hit something hard beneath a bush. He put the flashlight beam right on it.

"Hey guys, come here," he said. "I think the moose ate some kind of animal. This looks like a…I think it's a... a bone."

They bent down.

"Moose don't eat animals," said Bridget.

A piece of bone was sticking up out of the dirt.

"I don't think that's something the moose got anyway," replied Willie. "A moose couldn't bury it and it's in there pretty deep."

"Okay," said Peter, "let's dig it out."

They started scraping around the bone with their hands, while the girls looked back and forth at each other. Bridget raised her eyebrows and Anna shrugged her shoulders. Gracey squirmed. They knew that a moose hadn't been around.

"What do you think it is?" Bridget whispered.

Anna stood up. "Let's just go, guys, we don't need to be digging up any old bones," she said loudly.

She shone her flashlight nervously around the area to make sure no animals were lurking around.

"This is research," Charlie said importantly. "We could be making a discovery about moose."

"This is crazy!" Bridget and Anna cried in unison.

"I'm scared," Gracey said. "And hungry. Let's go. There's no moose, guys. It was just a trick."

"Yeah, sure," said Charlie. "You just want to go back to camp."

Suddenly Anna's flashlight stopped moving. She tugged on Bridget's arm.

"What's that?" she whispered, pointing nearby.

"Where?" asked Bridget.

"There—it's partly buried," said Anna, pointing again.

Peter came over and moved slowly through the leaves toward what looked like a long branch with a handle on it.

"Okay," he said nervously. "It's definitely not a snake, but it's not just a branch either. Keep the light on it, Anna."

He pulled his sleeve over his hand so he wouldn't have to touch it with bare hands, leaned down and quickly jerked it from the pile of leaves. Anna shone her light on it. She helped Peter brush off the thick dirt that was clinging to it.

They stared down at a long, weathered stick with carvings on it, and a knob on the top.

"It looks like an old walking stick!" said Bridget. "My grandfather has one like that."

"Well, what's it doing way out here?" Anna asked. "This is giving me the creeps."

"Yeah," said Bridget. "Let's just go. Now."

Just then Charlie and Willie bolted upright from their squatting positions, their hands and forearms covered with dirt, and screamed so loudly

Bridget thought she felt the trees shake.

“Aaaaaggggghhhhh! It’s a skeleton! A foot!!” Charlie hollered, “Run!”

“Aaaggghhhhh!” they all started screaming at once. They raced through the bushes, thrashing through branches, and tripping over logs to get back to their campsite.

Chapter Seven

Bony Tales

They screamed until they got to the trail, where Bridget's mom and Mrs. Bends were running toward them.

"What's the matter?" Bridget's mom shouted, holding out her arms.

"Is someone hurt?" asked Mrs. Bends.

"N-n-nobody," said Willie. "But somebody was hurt, before…"

"Who? What do you mean, hurt before? Before what? What's happened?" his mother asked in a rush of words.

Everybody started talking at once, in bits and pieces, flailing their arms and pointing toward the woods.

"All right, what's going on?" Bridget's mom asked. "One at a time. And first of all, why were you off the trail? We talked about this earlier today."

"We were following moose tracks…" Willie started to say, his voice shaking.

"There's no moose," Bridget said, and then burst out crying. "We were playing a joke. We made the tracks."

"What? That's crazy," said Charlie. "Well, moose or no moose, there's a FOOT in the woods. A real foot from a real person."

"F-f-from a PERSON," Willie agreed.

"What?" asked Bridget's mom.

"The boys dug up the skeleton of a foot," said Bridget. "We were all in the woods and the boys were looking for signs of a moose. Remember I told you we were going to trick them into thinking a moose had been around?"

"And look at this," Anna said, holding out the stick, her hands shaking. "It's a walking stick. It must've belonged to that person."

Charlie took the stick, his eyes popping wide now that he could see the intricate carvings in the wood.

"This is one sweet walking stick," he said, turning it over in his hands.

"Where's my mom?" Gracey asked, and then she burst out crying.

Bridget's mom gave her a hug.

"Your mom's back at the campsite with Gretchen. We'll go back there in a few minutes. But first we need to see what's going on here. Okay?"

"Okay," agreed Gracey, sniffling.

"You girls are sissies," said Charlie.

"That's enough of that kind of talk, young man," scolded his mom.

"Yeah, you were screaming back there, too, skunk tail," said Bridget. "And you're the one that hollered for us to run, so there."

"Okay, everybody, calm down. We need you guys to show us where you found the foot."

"Charlie, did you touch it?" his mother asked.

"Yeah," he said. "But I didn't know what it was."

"Well, you make sure and scrub your hands when we get back to the campsite," she said. "Now let's go see what this is all about."

They all walked slowly back to where the bushes were broken down, and Willie pointed the flashlight.

"In there," he said.

Gracey clutched Bridget's hand.

"I'm not going back in there, no way."

"I'll stay here with whoever doesn't want to go," said Bridget's mom.

Bridget went with Mrs. Bends, Anna, Charlie, Willie, and Peter. She was frightened, but she had to see for herself or she knew she'd always wonder about this strange discovery. She tried to imagine herself as a character in one of the mystery books she was always reading; someone who would surely be brave enough to investigate a mystery like this. After all, it was just bones, right, she kept telling herself.

They pushed aside the bushes slowly, walking carefully, with Mrs. Bends in front shining her flashlight. Each time Bridget stepped on a twig and it cracked, she jumped back, looking around, thinking someone else was there in the forest. Her whole insides were wiggling.

"This is crazy," whispered Anna.

"Shhh!" hissed Willie.

"Hey, it's not like he can hear us," Charlie said. "He's dead, get it?"

Why did he have to say it like that? Bridget wondered. And what was she doing, walking toward a dead person?

But Bridget noticed that for all his tough words, Charlie was walking less than a full step behind his mother. Somehow, knowing they were probably all scared made it a bit easier to keep going.

They found the spot without difficulty and there it was, the dirty white skeleton of a foot sticking up out of the ground at an odd angle.

"Uh!" Bridget cried, sucking in her breath, and wrapping her arm around Anna, who was standing next to her.

"Oh," said Anna. "This is soooo creepy."

Mrs. Bends moved closer and peered down.

"There's definitely more here than just a foot," she said, sweeping the flashlight along the ground. "You can tell by the angle, it's connected to something, most likely a leg. And see how the ground looks so different here? It's more raised up than the area around it. I'd say there's probably a whole body under there."

"Let's go!" said Anna. "Now!"

"Hey, we brought our camping shovel for covering up the fire with dirt before we go to sleep. Maybe we could use it to dig up the rest of the body," said Charlie excitedly.

"NO WAY!" Bridget and Anna screamed at once.

"I'm outta' here," Peter said. "This is nuts. I don't want to see a dead body!"

"Nobody's doing any digging," said Mrs. Bends. "This is a job for the police to investigate."

"I can't believe this is really happening!" cried Bridget, staring at the spot, wanting to leave but afraid to turn around.

"Look, you guys made an important discovery. You could be helping with a long unsolved mystery," Mrs. Bends said.

Bridget managed a weak smile.

"If we ever get out of here, you have your own mystery to write," said Anna.

"Now, Willie, take off that Boy Scout bandana from around your neck so we can tie it around this little tree in front of the skeleton. This way the police will be able to find it."

Willie reluctantly took off his bandana. He loved to wear it because it showed everyone he was a Boy Scout. He was always doing things with his troop, and he had earned enough honors so that next week he was going to a big Scout jamboree over the long holiday weekend.

"It's okay; I'll get you another bandana in time for the jamboree," promised his mom. "And just think of the story you'll have to tell the guys in your troop."

Willie smiled and handed her the bandana. She wrapped it around the sapling.

"Put one of your Boy Scout knots in it to make sure it holds," said his mom, and Willie did.

"Come on, let's get to the campsite. There's a fire started. Mrs. Hull is back there with Gretchen and she'll be getting worried," said Mrs. Bends.

Just then one of the larger trees seemed to groan as the wind came up and one of its branches rubbed against another branch overhead.

"What's that?" Anna shouted.

Startled, they all looked up, nervous to see what the noise was.

"It's just the wind in the trees," said Mrs. Bends.

"It, um, it looks like arms waving around up there," Peter said, and at the mention of another body part, they all just turned and ran back toward the trail as fast as they could without another word, crashing through the bushes as they went.

Chapter Eight

Ghost Stories

"I'm so glad you guys are back," said Gracey. "We didn't like waiting for you all alone out here, did we Mrs. Meagher?"

"No," answered Bridget's mom. "What did you find?"

"Well, it's definitely a foot, and it's attached to something. It looks like there's possibly an entire skeleton buried beneath dirt and leaves. We marked the spot with Willie's bandana so the police can find it," said Mrs. Bends, putting her arm around her boys.

Anna's mom smiled and hugged her girls.

"Oh, I'm so glad you're all safely back."

They told her the whole story while they stood around the fire, very close to each other. Bridget couldn't stop shaking. The sun was newly set, and the campfire cast an eerie orange glow on their faces.

"What do we do now?" Bridget asked urgently, her eyebrows arched like the peak of a mountain. "Where are all the flashlights, Mom? We have to go back down the mountain. We can't stay here with a dead person!"

Bridget's mom pulled Bridget to her, and ran her hands through her daughter's hair. "Let's all just stay calm now."

"Maybe the moose got the dead person!" Willie said.

"Moose don't eat meat!" said Anna. "Besides, that foot was buried for a while, and plus, there was no moose. That was our plan to trick you guys."

"Oh, ha ha, very funny," Charlie replied. "Look what happened."

"What happened is you touched a dead foot!" said Bridget, shaking her head.

"Do you think maybe the person fell and got trapped, like under a rock?" Gracey asked.

"Maybe he got attacked by a wild animal. We could be next." Peter hopped up and down nervously. "We have to get out of here."

"Listen, gang, we don't have any answers right now," said Mrs. Bends. "Let's just think about this and get something to eat."

"Eat?" said Peter. "I can't eat right now. I'll puke! I'll never sleep either. Let's get out of here."

"Not gonna' happen," said Charlie. "You want to walk down this mountain at night in the dark, with dead people around?"

Gracey clutched her mom's arm. "There's MORE dead people?" she screamed.

"No, honey, no. Now look, nobody's going anywhere. It's not safe to hike down a mountain at night. Besides, our tents are all set up, we have a fire, and we're fine. Gretchen's asleep in the tent."

Nobody said anything. They all stared into the fire.

Suddenly, one of the partially-burnt logs that was propped up on a bigger one crashed down into the middle of the flames with a loud THUNK, sending sparks flying upward. Everyone jumped back and screamed.

"W-w-what if the dead person was murdered?" Willie blurted out.

Everyone's eyes got as round as the moon overhead.

"That's it. I'm going. Right now." Peter told them all. "This is crazy. We're on top of a mountain with a murderer. He could be hiding up in the fire tower."

"No way." Bridget declared. "They lock it. Sarah told me."

"Well, if he's a murderer he could break a lock!" exclaimed Charlie. "Duh!"

"You guys, come on now," insisted Bridget's mom. "I'll tell you what. I'm going to get some flashlights. Boys, you go in your tent and get yours too."

"I'm not walking over there," stated Willie.

"Come on," said Charlie. "I'll go." He stared at his brother.

"Go ahead," Willie said. "What if the murderer is in the tent?"

"BOYS!" yelled Mrs. Bends. "There is no murderer on top of this mountain. I'll go with Mrs. Meagher and get the flashlights, so everyone can have their own, and we'll just stay by the fire."

"I wish I would've brought Simon," Peter said, looking at Ming. "At least we could've had one dog for the boys and one for the girls. And the dogs would bark if someone snuck up on us."

"Well, why didn't you bring him?" Charlie asked. "We sure could use him right now."

"My scaredy-cat sister wanted to keep him this weekend for a sleep-over in the BACKYARD. Sure, here I am on a mountain with a murderer and she's got the dog in the backyard at a stupid sleepover."

Mrs. Bends and Mrs. Meagher came back with the flashlights, and told everyone to sit on some logs by the fire.

"I'm sure it was probably some hiker that was lost up here years ago," Mrs. Meagher said. "Thing's decay at different times in different climates. Someone will be able to figure out how long this person has been here by how much the body has decomposed."

"Do you think the rest of the body is there, too?" Anna asked.

"I don't know and I'm not going to look!" answered Bridget.

"It all depends on how long it's been there or if animals carried some parts of it away," her mom said.

"But except for the walking stick, which people might not remember, how will they ever know who it was, or how they died?" Charlie asked her.

"Well, the foot you guys uncovered today will probably be enough to tell. "Diseases and injuries can leave markings on bones while a person is alive, like etchings or carvings, and that can reveal a lot about an identity. There's also DNA testing now to help identify people."

"How do you know so much about this, Mrs. Meagher?" asked Willie.

"Well, Joe, the guy I'm dating, is a professor of anthropology. He's done work in this area. He's even helped police to identify a body before."

Bridget looked up at her mom. "I didn't know he did all that," she exclaimed. "That's pretty cool."

Her mom gave her a smile.

"How about when we get home, I'll have Joe over for dinner, and all you guys can come so he can tell you about his work? Maybe the police will even ask him to help with this case."

"Cool," said Willie.

"You mean, 'groovy,' " said Anna, smiling at her mom. "Like the road sign."

"Yeah, and I'll bring the bones in for the next Show and Tell!" Charlie said.

"No way, Charlie," replied his mom. "Those bones have to be taken out of here by experts, so nothing is disturbed or broken. Remember, there may be more bones buried in the same spot; maybe even the rest of the body."

"I wouldn't touch those bones for anything," said Peter. "Charlie, you're just talking tough, you're as scared as we were. Remember, that's a real person's foot! And just think, the head might be there, too!"

Just then Gretchen woke up in the tent and started crying, and everyone started screaming all over again. Her mom went to bring her out by the fire and calm her down.

Then they all moved a little closer to each other. It was totally dark out now except for the glow of the flames, and the wind was picking up. The scent of balsam and pine spread through the night air. Every now and then the wind howled across the top of the mountain and Bridget was sure it sounded like a person who was about to be murdered.

Chapter Nine

The Wind Speaks

Everyone—the kids and the moms—piled into the two larger tents that were side by side, leaving the pup tent empty. They were all squished, but they didn't care. This time, they wanted to be touching the sleeping bag of the person next to them.

But no one could sleep. For hours, they lay awake and talked about the body and who it could possibly have been.

"I think it's a lost hiker and that's that," said Mrs. Bends.

"Or someone who was escaping from a prison?" Willie asked.

"Or someone who got in an argument with their husband or wife or boss, and just came up here to be alone? But suppose they didn't tell anyone where they were going? Then, when they never came home, their family would just think that person didn't care anymore and just left them. Wouldn't that be awful?" Bridget asked, and started to cry.

"I think you read a lot of books and get very imaginative ideas," her mom replied, stroking Bridget's hair. "I'm not saying that couldn't have happened, but chances are one of us moms would remember a story like that.

We've all grown up around here."

"But it could have been someone from out of town, out of this whole area!" Bridget said, propping herself up on her elbow. "No one here would know someone like that was missing."

"What if their leg got stuck under a log, and they called for help, but there were no fire rangers up here anymore, so they yelled all night and no one heard them and they finally died?" Charlie asked loudly from the next tent.

"It could be one of the fire rangers!" Willie exclaimed, sitting up next to his brother. "Maybe it was his last trip down the mountain, after they closed the cabin, and he never made it down."

The wind howled even louder and Gracey squished as close as she could to her mother.

"I want to go home," she said, and she began crying and hiccupping at the same time.

"Listen guys, it'll be morning before we know it, so no more talking. Let's get to sleep!" Mrs. Meagher said.

Bridget, with Ming tucked next to her in the sleeping bag, waited a while, and whispered, "Mom?"

"Yeah?" her mom whispered back.

"Well, um, there's something I have to tell you." Then she stopped, listening to her own breath, which sounded loud inside the small space of the tent. She could hear the trees and branches rustling in the wind.

"What is it?"

"Well, I, um, failed a big test in school. I've been really upset about it. And I didn't want to tell you or Dad, 'cause you always say how smart I am. I was really embarrassed," Bridget blurted out.

"So I've, well, I've just been studying like mad every night to make up for it. I guess I didn't know school would be so hard this year."

"I see," said her mom, whispering back in the dark. "Well, thanks for telling me. I wish you'd have told me sooner; I could've helped. It must have felt pretty bad. You are a good student, you know. Why do you think you failed?"

"Well, maybe," Bridget got quiet again. "I was spending a lot of time on the phone at night, talking with kids from school. I'm trying to make new friends."

"So, we'll have to limit that, okay?" Her mom gave her a squeeze, and Bridget was glad she did. The wind was sounding more and more creepy every minute.

"You probably want more time to talk to Joe on the phone anyway," Bridget offered, trying to find some way to talk about him.

Her mom laughed. "Well, I do like to use the phone SOMETIMES, you know. But this is about you right now. We'll figure out some time limits, okay? Then maybe, once you get your grades back on track, you can have your new friends over for a sleepover some weekend."

"Great idea," Bridget said. She was quiet for awhile, and then she blurted out, "One more thing, Mom, could you not call Joe your boyfriend? It's too weird. He's not a boy. I'm the one that's supposed to be having boyfriends soon…"

"We'll talk about YOUR dating later," replied her mom. "That's a big discussion. As for Joe, well, I really enjoy his company. I guess 'boyfriend' is a pretty silly word for adults. I'll have to think on that one, okay?"

"Okay," answered Bridget, listening to the sound of the tent as it flapped back and forth in the wind. "But I still wish you and Dad were together. I wish he was here right now," she said, her voice shaking. "It wouldn't be so scary."

Her mother reached down into the bottom of her sleeping bag.

"I thought you might miss your dad, so I brought this along, just in case. I didn't show you earlier in front of the boys because I thought they might tease you. But who cares anyway, right?"

She turned on her little flashlight, and held up Lester, Bridget's favorite bear that her father had given her when he and her mom got divorced.

"Now you can sleep with Ming and Lester," said her mom.

"Thanks, Mom." Bridget could feel her mom's smile steady the darkness. She took Lester, and tucked the bear and her flashlight under one arm, and Ming under the other.

Outside, the wind picked up, shaking the tent and howling, awoooooo, and this time Bridget thought it sounded like the voice of a ghost wandering around looking for a missing foot.

Chapter Ten

Fire

In the middle of dreaming about a bony old man rattling the tent, Bridget woke up suddenly, her eyes wide and her heart thumping inside her sweatshirt like bumper cars being rammed into each other. She was covered with sweat. Ming was growling, and Bridget heard loud snapping noises. She could see tiny orange lights outside the tent.

Her throat was so dry she couldn't even scream. She didn't know if she was dreaming or not, but then, why was Ming growling?

Suddenly, she remembered the sign at the end of the road to Mt. Arab.

DEAD END.

That's when she sat up, and started yelling.

"Get up, everyone! We're all going to die! This is our dead end. Look! Something's out there! It's coming to get us!"

Everyone yanked themselves out of their sleeping bags and rushed outside the tents. Gretchen started crying and her mother held her close.

Pop! Pop! Bang! They could hear noises coming from a backpack not far from where they had made their fire, and there were flames near it!

"Quick, throw dirt on it!" shouted Mrs. Bends. "Willie, Charlie, get the camp shovel. Hurry!"

Willie grabbed the small shovel they had used to dig a trench around the fire pit earlier in the night and began throwing dirt on the flames. Charlie and Peter dug up dirt with their hands and threw it on the fire and on the backpack. Ming raced around, barking.

Anna grabbed their water jug and doused the flames with water.

Thick smoke billowed around them as the fire hissed while it went out. It smelled worse than smelly old socks.

Mrs. Bends finally sat on a log and put her head in her hands.

"What a night!" she said. "Whose backpack was that?"

"Mine," answered Peter, hanging his head.

"What was in it?"

"Um, firecrackers."

"Yeah," said Charlie, "He had some left over from the Fourth of July. See, this was our trick, because we knew the girls would have one, too. You know how Peter wore that hat with the lights? That was the clue. Since you guys are always looking for clues in signs and stuff."

"What clue?" asked Mrs. Bends, looking more confused than ever.

"A clue that something was going to happen like on the Fourth of July," said Willie. "We were going to sneak out of our tents at night and light the firecrackers outside the girls' tent."

"But with everything that happened, I forgot all about our plan," Peter said. "I don't know what happened just now."

"It looks like we were all so worried about the foot, we didn't put out the fire as carefully as we usually do," said Mrs. Bends. "With it being so windy tonight, it must have blown on some coals and restarted the fire, or else some sparks flew out and landed right on your backpack, setting off the firecrackers."

"Well, I guess we're lucky the firecrackers were there, actually," said Bridget, her voice raspy from shouting. "That's what woke Ming up, then me. Otherwise the fire might have spread."

Willie used the shovel to break up the rest of the coals in the fire, and then threw more dirt on them. Anna poured the rest of the water onto the sooty pile.

"I thought for sure that those noises and those lights were the ghost of that skeleton," said Charlie.

"Me, too," Peter added.

"Was your tent rattling in the wind, too?" asked Willie.

"Yeah," said Bridget, shivering, "and some of the heavy tree branches rubbed against each other and groaned all night, too."

"I think this is the longest night of my life," said Anna.

"Me, too," agreed her mom, rocking Gretchen in her arms.

"I'm never telling any ghost stories again," announced Gracey, shaking her head. "But I'm starving. Can we have something to eat?"

Mrs. Meagher yawned.

"Well, it's not quite morning yet, but I guess we can pretend. How about some peanut butter and jelly sandwiches on pita bread, gang?"

"Great, I'm hungry too," said Peter. "And, I'm, uh, sorry about the firecrackers."

"Your backpack sure is ruined," said Mrs. Hull, pointing to the blackened mess on the side of the fire.

"Actually, it's my sister's. I lost mine this summer. I'll probably have to do her chores for a couple weeks now to make up for this," Peter groaned.

"Well, start with a chore here. You can slice open the pita bread. Willie, you put on the peanut butter, and I'll put on the jam," said Mrs. Meagher. "Charlie, find us some knives."

They sat around what once was their fire and ate their sandwiches. Nearly all of them had soot on their faces and ashes in their hair. No one seemed to care. They ate some apples. Then they ate some candy bars. A squirrel scampered around, looking for crumbs. Bridget fed Ming. They sat up eating and talking for so long that pretty soon a faint light came into the sky. Some birds started singing.

Peter jumped up first, his pants covered in grime.

"Now can we go home?" he asked.

Chapter Eleven

Trail Markers

"Well, I guess we'll never get back to sleep anyway," answered Mrs. Meagher. "Although I'll tell you, I'm going to take one big long nap when we get home."

"By the time we get all the tents down and pack up our gear, it will be daylight," said Mrs. Bends. "So let's go. We might as well."

They all raced around and started taking the stakes out of the tents and rolling up their sleeping bags. Bridget never felt so happy to be thinking about climbing down a mountain in her life.

"Hey, wait a minute," said her mom. "We need something to mark off the trail near the area where you guys found the skeleton, so the authorities will see Willie's bandana and know right where to look when we send them up here later today."

"I'm not going near that place!" said Anna.

"Well, we walk right by it on our way down the mountain. Chances are that poor soul just got off the trail, because it's not that far into the woods. So what can we use?" asked Mrs. Bends.

"See, we need those trail markers I was talking about!" said Gracey. "Then we could make a sign."

"We can use the little flag we made from my T-shirt and a stick, before, when we got to the top of the mountain," Peter suggested.

"Good idea," replied Mrs. Hull.

They finished loading their stuff, stomped on the fire again and shoveled dirt on it a few more times to be sure it was really out.

Mrs. Hull put Gretchen in her backpack, and hoisted it up on her shoulders.

Charlie picked up the walking stick and turned it around over and over in his hands. In the daylight, he could see the detailed carvings that circled the stick. There was a beaver, a red-tailed hawk, and a bald eagle. On the other side there was a great blue heron and a doe.

"Wow," he said. "I sure do love this."

"I bet whoever used this walking stick would carve animals onto it that he saw on his different hikes. Or actually, maybe it was a she," Bridget said. "Who knows? But I do know that walking stick is telling us a story."

"We're going to have to drop it off to the State Police on the way home today," said her mom. "This is very important. We must report it right away. The stick and the bones are all clues to help the police, coroners, pathologists, and even anthropologists find out who this person was and how they died. Then maybe, finally, some family somewhere can have some peace."

"So I guess we're part of the discovery team," said Charlie, putting on his fur hat with the skunk tail. "And for right now, I'm gonna' walk down the mountain using this walking stick. And then I'm going to find a stick of my own and sandpaper it and everything, and start carving stuff that I've seen."

"Me, too," said Willie. "We'll have twin Irish walking sticks!"

The two brothers were born less than a year apart, so their parents called them "Irish twins."

They started down the trail, and when they got to the spot where they saw a lot of the bushes trampled, they knew that's where they had rushed out of the woods the night before.

Bridget piled a bunch of rocks together on the side of the trail to make a cairn, something hikers use to leave other hikers a message, or to signal the way when there are no trail markers. Then Peter planted the flag on the trail.

As they headed down the mountain, they talked more about who the mysterious person might have been.

"I can't wait to hear Joe explain just how they'll figure out who this is," said Bridget.

"It may take a while to track everything down. There'll be a lot of lab work and other types of things," cautioned Mrs. Meagher.

"Well, in the meantime, I think I'll write a story about who it might be and how they got on top of Mt. Arab," said Bridget. "It will be an original school project, that's for sure. Maybe I can get extra credit."

Charlie, proudly leading the group with the walking stick, stopped and turned back to Bridget.

"You can write a story, but I'm gonna' tell one with my walking stick. The first thing I'm gonna' carve on my stick is the skeleton of the foot, that I saw and touched."

"A fire tower!" Willie said, breaking into a sooty smile. "That's what I'm going to put on my stick first. To show we climbed all the mountains with fire towers on them in the Adirondacks."

"I'm going to make a walking stick, too," Peter added. "And I'm going to put a moose on mine!"

"You can't!" said Anna. "You never saw one."

"Then I'll just carve moose tracks," replied Peter. "I saw some of those, even if they weren't real."

"You should carve an exploding backpack on your walking stick," laughed Gracey, her eyes twinkling.

"Well, guys, I'll tell you what," said Bridget. "I'm going to find myself an *elaborate* walking stick."

"Here come Bridget's fancy words again," said Anna. "Watch out."

She held onto her younger sister's arm as they climbed over a spot in the trail that was wet from a trickle of water and mushy leaves.

"Let's find some good sticks on the way down the mountain," Anna suggested.

"No! Please! Let's wait until we get home and look in the woods there," said Gracey. "I don't want to find any more skeletons around here. I just wanna' go home."

"Okay," said Anna to her little sister. "It's a deal. On the way down, we can think about what we want to carve on our sticks. And I was thinking, I'm going to do a search on the Internet to see if I can find out about missing persons in the Adirondacks. That might help us discover who this person is."

"Good idea," said Bridget. "Let's work on it together. I bet we can both get a school project going from this."

Anna smiled at Bridget.

Everyone was eager to get home, and they walked quickly down the trail. Gretchen bounced along in the backpack, sound asleep against her mother's back. Ming scampered down the trail, sniffing everything along the way and kicking up leaves with her paws.

As she headed downhill, Bridget thought and thought about what she could put on her walking stick. This was going to be a fun project. She held onto a tree as she walked carefully down a steep part, her eyes still darting into the woods to be sure there weren't any more skeletons, or any killers running around.

As they neared the bottom of the trail, they all started running to the end of the path.

Then Bridget shouted, "Wait! I've got it! I know the first thing I'm going to carve on my walking stick, once I get one."

"What?" asked Anna, "A dictionary?"

They all burst out laughing.

"No, a road sign that will tell all about our trip," replied Bridget, pointing down the road. "It's going to say DEAD END."

About the Author

Liza Frenette has hiked Mount Arab many times, and she was usually the last one to make it to the top. She is a native of Tupper Lake, former resident of Saranac Lake, and now lives in Albany, N.Y.

This is her third book in the series about the adventures of a group of kids growing up in the Adirondacks. *Soft Shoulders*, which was published in 1999, won a national writing award from The Writer's Voice of Silver Bay. It was followed by *Dangerous Falls Ahead*, published in 2001, also by North Country Books. You can read more about the author at www.lizafrenette.com